Words to Know Before You Read

championship

outfield

pitcher

scores

strike

tough

www.rourkepublishing.com

Edited by Luana K. Mitten
Illustrated by Bob Reese
Art Direction and Page Layout by Renee Brady

Library of Congress Cataloging-in-Publication Data

Karapetkova, Holly
 Hoots on First? / Holly Karapetkova.
     p. cm. -- (Little Birdie Books)
 ISBN 978-1-61741-817-4 (hard cover) (alk. paper)
 ISBN 978-1-61236-021-8 (soft cover)
 Library of Congress Control Number: 2011924694

Rourke Publishing
Printed in the United States of America, North Mankato, Minnesota
060711
060711CL

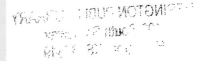

www.rourkepublishing.com - rourke@rourkepublishing.com
Post Office Box 643328 Vero Beach, Florida 32964

Hoot's on First?

By Holly Karapetkova

Illustrated by Bob Reese

Today is the big game. The Forest Animals play the Swamp Animals for the Little League Championship.

Hoot the Owl and Woody the Beaver play for the Forest Animals. Hoot plays first base. Woody plays the outfield. They love baseball.

The Swamp Animals look tough.

"Do you think we can win, Hoot?" asks Honey the Bear. Honey is the pitcher for the Forest Animals.

"I don't know," Hoot says. "The Swamp Animals are good, but we're good, too."

It's time to start the game.
Honey pitches the first ball.
It's a strike!

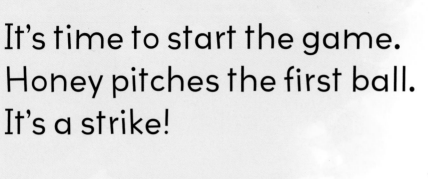

13

At the end of the game, the Forest Animals and the Swamp Animals are tied, one to one. Hoot is up at bat. Bam! He hits the ball. Hoot's on first!

15

Now Woody is up at bat. He hits the ball and runs to first. Hoot's on second!

Finally, it's Honey's turn. She hits the ball hard. Hoot runs to third base. Then he runs across home plate. Hoot scores! The Forest Animals win the championship.

"Congratulations," the Swamp Animals say. "You guys are *REALLY* good."

"So are you," Hoot says, "and you played a great game!"

After Reading Activities

You and the Story...

What teams are playing baseball?

Who scores the winning run?

At the end of the game how did the winners show good sportsmanship? How did the losers show good sportsmanship?

Tell how you can show good sportsmanship on the playground at school.

Words You Know Now...

Using the words listed below, find two compound words and write them on a piece of paper.

Then find two words with ou in them and write them on your paper. Do you know any other words that have the ou sound in them? Write them on your paper, too.

championship   pitcher   strike

outfield   scores   tough

You Could... Plan A Game At School

- Decide what game you want to organize.

- What rules do you have to know to play the game?

- Who will you invite to play this game with you?

- Decide who will be on each team.

- How will you keep score?

About the Author

Holly Karapetkova lives in Arlington, VA., with her family and two dogs. She likes watching her son play baseball, and she loves writing books for kids.

About the Illustrator

Bob Reese began his art career at age 17 working for Walt Disney. His projects included the animated feature films Sleeping Beauty, The Sword and the Stone, and Paul Bunyan. He has also worked for Bob Clampett and Hanna Barbera Studios. He resides in Utah and enjoys spending time with his two daughters, five grandchildren, and cat named Venus.